Grover's Own ALPHABET

A GOLDEN BOOK • NEW YORK

 Published in the United States by Golden Books, an imprint of Random House Children's Books, a division of Penguin Random House LLC, 1745 Broadway, New York, NY 10019, and in Canada by Penguin Random House Canada Limited, Toronto, in conjunction with Sesame Workshop. Golden Books, A Golden Book, A Little Golden Book, the G colophon, and the distinctive gold spine are registered trademarks of Penguin Random House LLC.
Visit us on the Web!
rhcbooks.com
SesameStreetBooks.com
www.sesamestreet.org
Educators and librarians, for a variety of teaching tools, visit us at RHTeachersLibrarians.com
ISBN 978-1-9848-4793-5 (trade) — ISBN 978-1-9848-4794-2 (ebook)
Printed in the United States of America
10 9 8 7 6 5 4 3
Random House Children's Books supports the First Amendment and celebrates the right to read.

A

This is a little awkward, but is it not an *absolutely* adorable A?

B

I bet you think making this big beautiful B with my furry little body is easy. Well, it is not!

And now I am making you a **cute** letter C! But I am not very comfortable.

It is not such a big deal to do a D! It is **delightful**!

E

I have to bend my **elbow** exactly right,
but how is this for an elegant E? EEEK!

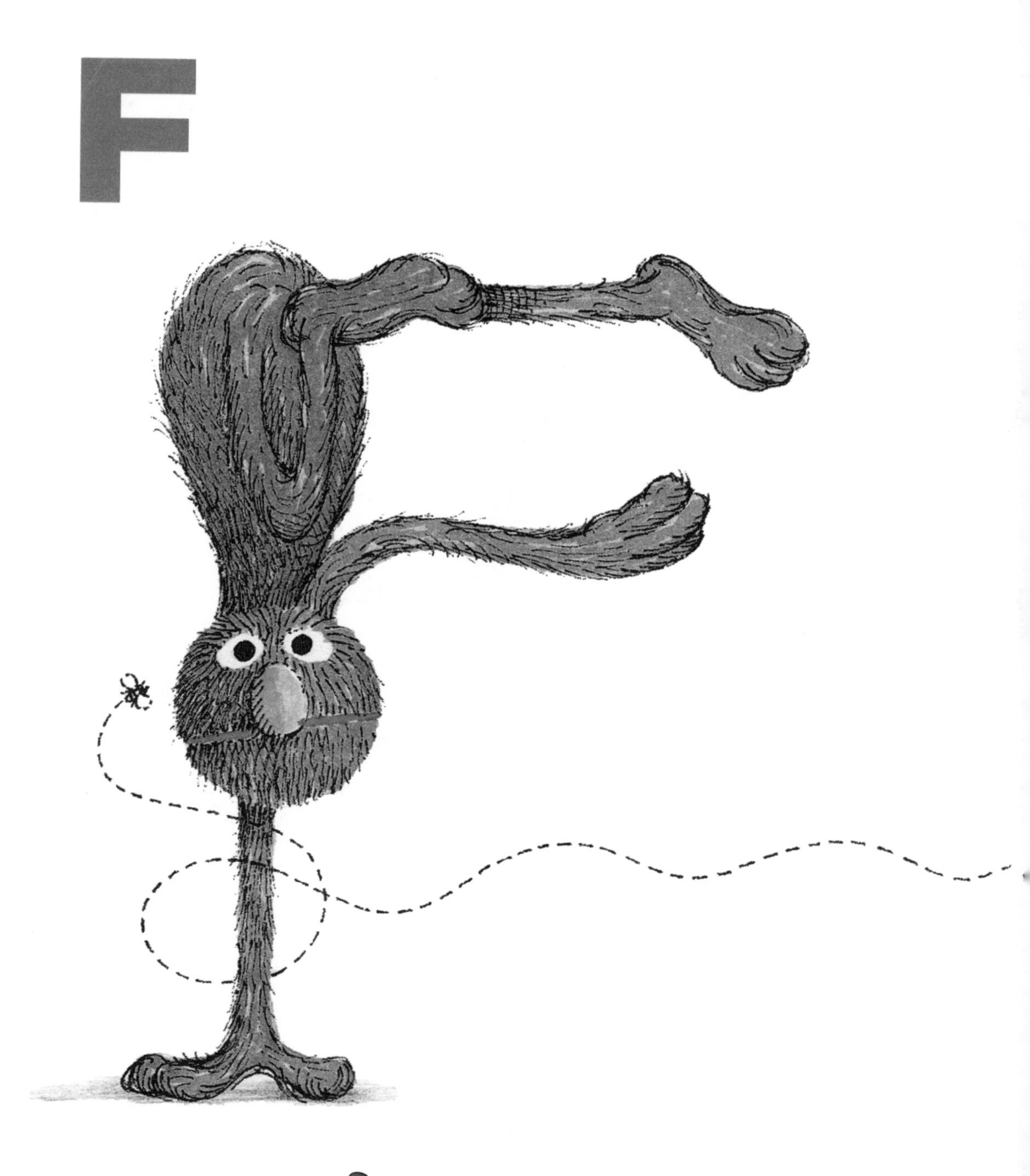

Here is a **funny**, furry F for you!

G is for **GROVER**! Watch while I, Grover, form the great letter G! Am I not graceful?

H

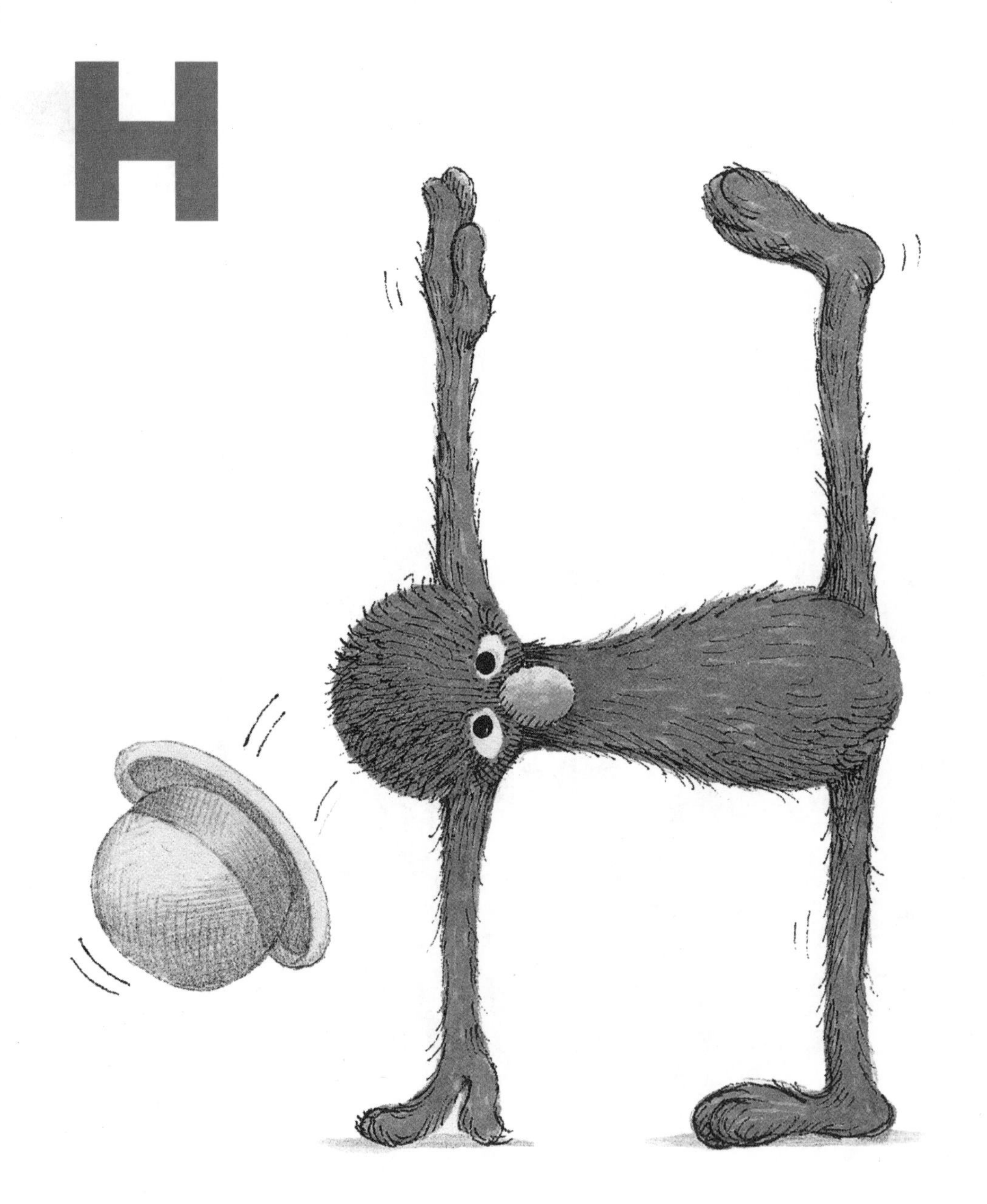

I hope this H makes you happy. It is hard to do (pant, pant!). Help!

It is I, Grover, making the **important** letter I.

J

Now (puff, puff!) I am **juggling** just to show you a J. I could get in a jam this way.

K

This is the letter K. I am not **kidding**.

I do not like to be lazy about this, but the lovely letter L takes very little work.

Is this not a magnificent M? It is made by ME!

I thought we would **never** get to the nifty letter N!

Oh, my goodness (glub, glub!). I am
not the only one in this **ocean**.

What is the point of my standing like this?
I am pretending to be the letter P.

Quick! Answer this question!
What letter am I now? Q?
Oh, thank goodness you guessed it.

R

You want an R? All RIGHT!! Here you are (pant, pant!). This is getting **ridiculous**!

S

So **sorry**. I could not find a single thing to assist me with this S. I simply had to use myself.

T

I have tried to make a **terrific** T for you! But, oh, I am so tired. TA-DA!

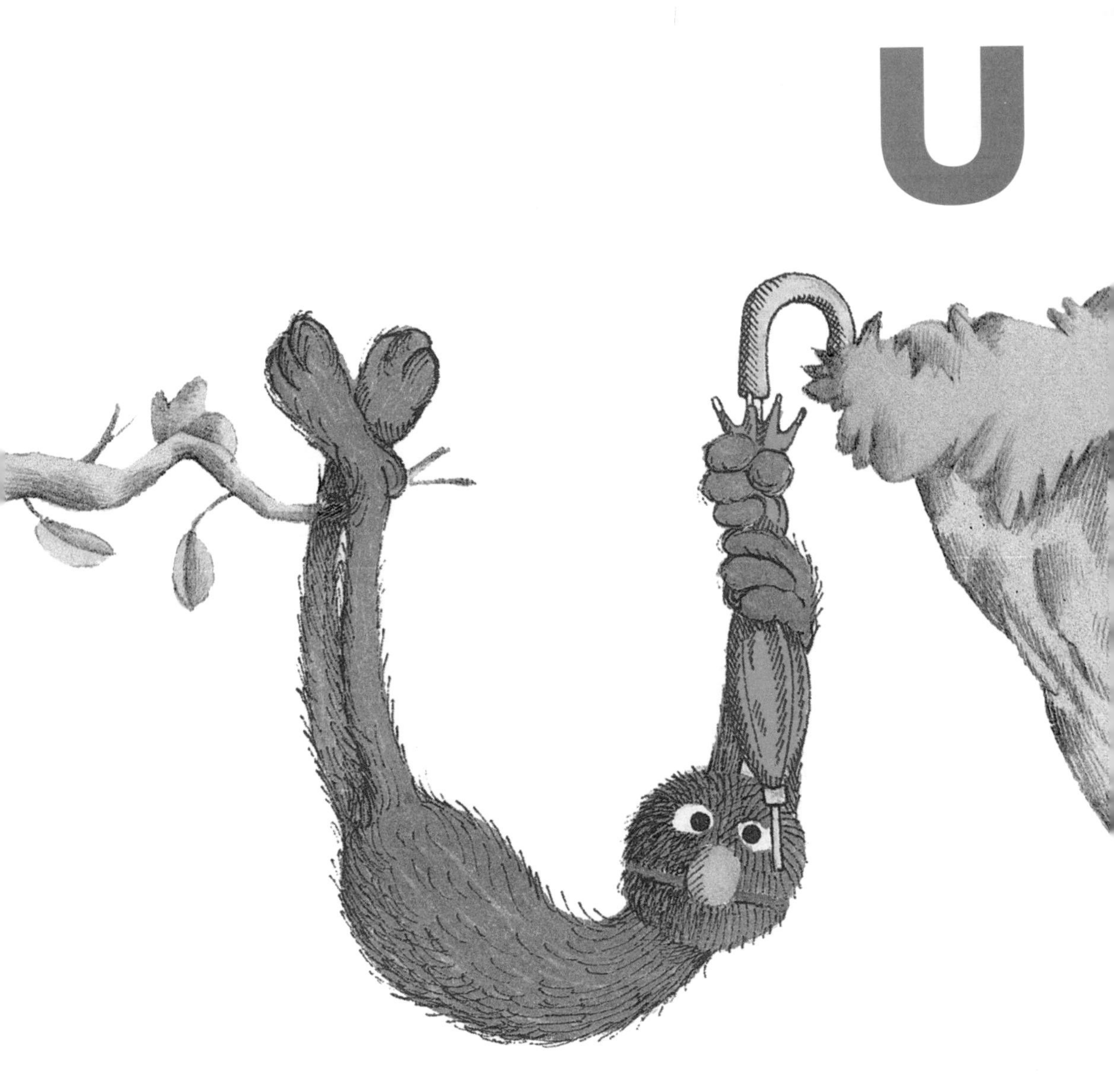

I would **undergo** anything to show you the letter U.

V

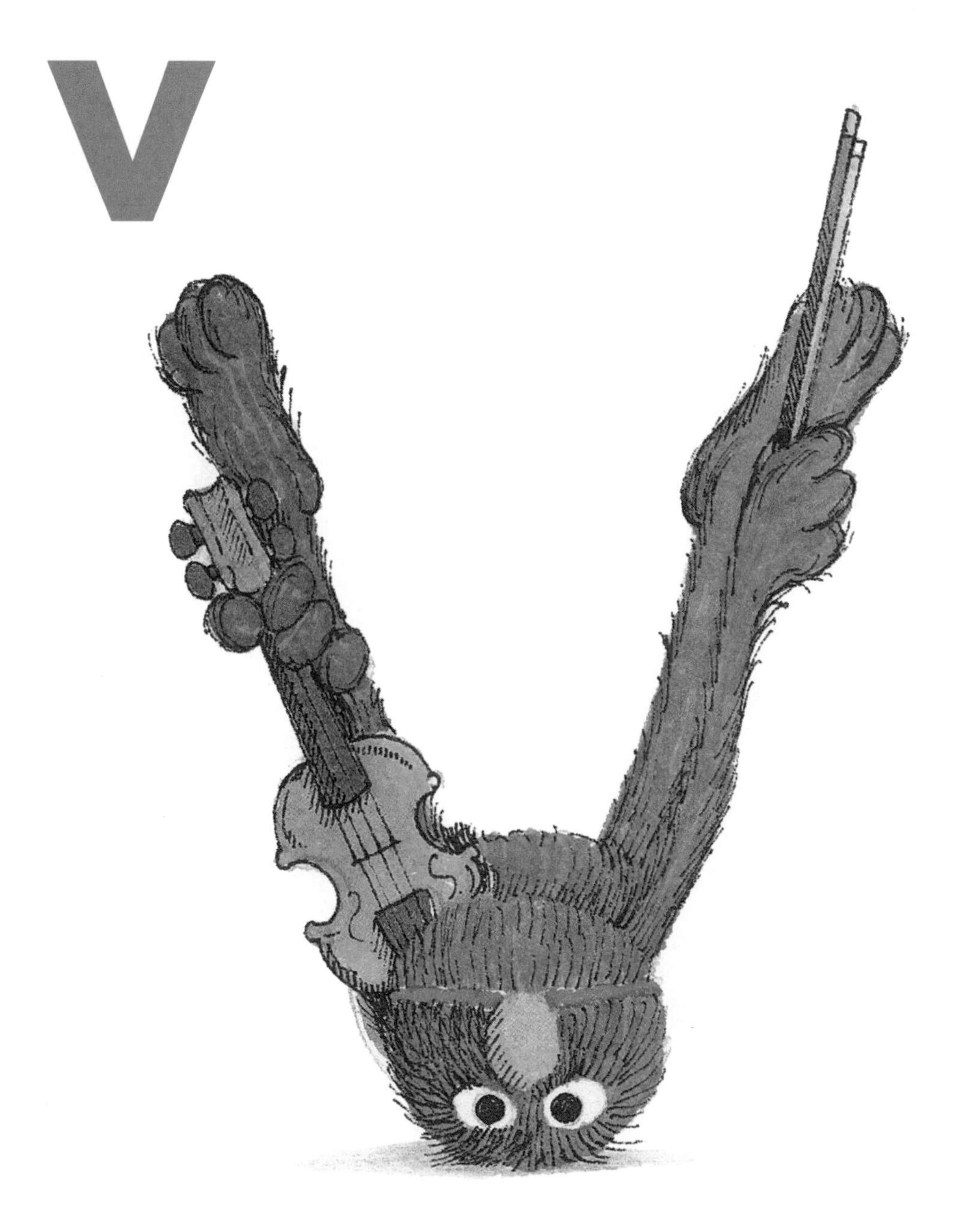

You are invited to view my very **valuable** letter V.

I wish you would watch my
wonderful diving W!

X

And how about this extraordinary X?
Oh, I am so excited!

Y
You, yes, you asked for it—the letter Y!
Yikes!

Z

Here it is (puff, puff!), the last letter–Z!
Did you like the way I zipped
through the entire alphabet?

This is not a letter of the alphabet.
This is a tired monster!